Thomas B. Brown

Thoughts Suggested by the Perusal of Gilfillan

and other authors, on the Sabbath

Thomas B. Brown

Thoughts Suggested by the Perusal of Gilfillan
and other authors, on the Sabbath

ISBN/EAN: 9783337378882

Printed in Europe, USA, Canada, Australia, Japan

Cover: Foto ©Andreas Hilbeck / pixelio.de

More available books at **www.hansebooks.com**

THOUGHTS

SUGGESTED BY

THE PERUSAL OF GILFILLAN,

AND OTHER AUTHORS,

ON THE

SABBATH.

BY

REV. THOMAS B. BROWN,

Pastor of the Seventh-Day Baptist Church at Little Genesee, N. Y.

SECOND EDITION.

ALFRED CENTER, N. Y.:

PUBLISHED BY THE AMERICAN SABBATH TRACT
SOCIETY,

A. H. LEWIS, AGENT.

1869.

PREFACE.

If it should be said that the writer of the following remarks was not brought up in the observance of the Bible Sabbath, but was rigidly trained in the notion that the first day of the week is holy time under the gospel, it would weigh nothing with many readers. With others, it might possibly awaken curiosity to see whether a person, who had renounced an observance so important to the interests of religion and humanity as the Sunday festival is supposed to be, could be entitled to any consideration as a man of cleverness. But the writer would simply say, let the question at issue be tested by the Scripture of truth, and if the reader shall then become satisfied that the seventh day, the last day of the week, is the only Sabbath divinely authorized

—a supposition not over and above absurd— he need give himself no trouble whether this little book is the production of a wise man or a fool.

One thing, certainly, is worthy of his attention: that weak-headed persons have souls, to be saved or lost, as well as the wise and prudent; they have an obedience to render, as well as the most intelligent and quick-sighted; and the presumption is, that the will of God is set forth in terms adapted to their weakness, and not in that obscure and inferential way which requires the aid of logic for its interpretation. If the simple language of the Bible, "The seventh day is the Sabbath of the Lord thy God," conveys to plain unsophisticated minds that the last day of the week is the appointed rest-day for mankind; if such language is what the most ignorant can understand without difficulty; while the idea of the sacred character of the first day, under the gospel, is no where distinctly set forth, and the process by which the idea acquires a seeming plausibility is one which can be understood, and clearly stated, only by those who have some compass of intellect: can there be any doubt in which direction lies the path of obedience? Therefore, if the observer of the seventh day can point to chapter and verse for his practice, and say, "Thus saith the Lord," the fact that he is a person of humble parts, and quite unlearned, instead of being an argument against the correctness of his practice, is a strong presumption in its favor; while, on the other hand, the fact that all the wise and prudent, the mighty and noble, the wealthy and illustrious, are in the observance of the Sunday, is one of the poorest considerations that can be alleged in its defense.

For the Bible claims to be a revelation of God's will to man; but if its doctrines and duties were stated in such a way that only the higher order of minds could understand them, its claims to be a divine revelation would be destroyed at once. So any religious observance, which claims to rest upon divine authority, should be clear and obvious to the most common minds.

We who keep the seventh day may, ir the judgment of some, be but rustics in the world of letters, but we know that our institution has a Bible name, that it is enjoined upon us in clear and unmistakable terms, and enforced by such reasons as we can easily comprehend. The most illiterate among us can give a scriptural reason for his practice in Sabbath-keeping.

THOUGHTS ON THE SABBATH.

T is a remarkable fact, that the day set apart for the public worship of God by the majority of Christians—the first day of the week—is not regarded as a Sabbath, to any great extent, by unconverted men. With many it is a day of recreation or amusement, with some a day of business, with others a day of journeying; while but few, outside of the religious circle, consider themselves guilty of sin when they fail to regard the day as holy to the Lord. It is not as if they were guilty of lying, or theft, or adultery, or any other offense against the Moral Law; for then conscience does not fail to remind them that they are under condemnation.

This fact greatly troubles our religious teachers, and leads to organized efforts for the promotion of the sanctification of the day. They hold Conventions ; they form permanent Associations ; they issue books and tracts, and send out Agents to distribute them ; they invite distinguished men to lecture on the subject ; in short, they do every thing they can in the way of moral suasion to accomplish their end, to say nothing of their repeated attempts to invoke legislative aid.

Nevertheless, the evil does not abate, but rather increases. If a slight improvement is effected in some places, the evil spreads more widely elsewhere. If the people are restrained to-day, to-morrow they break out with renewed violence. What is accomplished one year, is lost, or more than lost, the next. On the whole, it is questionable whether the most ardent advocates of Sunday observance feel any great encouragement in their labors, or entertain any strong hopes for the future.

Does it ever occur to these earnest men to inquire into the rationale of this phenomenon? Why, after so much labor to bring about what they think would be a very desirable reformation, is their work such a failure? Why is there less real success in this, than in almost any other department of moral reform? Perhaps they think it is because of the obdurate wickedness of those upon whom their labor has been expended. They set them down as persons whose consciences are seared—regular candidates for perdition. Indeed, nothing is more common than for Sabbath-breakers (as they are called) to be denounced as the most hardened class of sinners.

There may be something in this; but it is, at least, worth while to inquire whether the failure may not be owing, in some degree, to a defect in the argument by which it is attempted to establish the obligation of keeping holy the first day of the week. If there is a defect here, the better plan would be to correct it. After that, if men will not render obedience, it will be time enough to call them sinners.

But here it will be opposed, that the most of those who refuse to keep holy the first day of the week are influenced, not so much by the weakness of the argument, as by a desire "to get rid of the Sabbath altogether," and that this is the reason why they are looked upon as a hardened class of sinners.

"If we should fail of proving that the day has been changed, it would not touch the other great question, in regard to the perpetuity of the Sabbath, which has been argued upon its own merits." "The day has either been changed, or it has not.

If it has been changed, they are bound to conform to that change. If it has not, then they are bound to keep the original, or seventh day. So that whether it has been changed or not, they are equally bound to keep one seventh part of time as holy, which is the very conclusion they wish to avoid."

This is President Humphrey's way of meeting the difficulty, and in this he is abundantly sustained by other writers on the same side of the question. They all maintain that the sabbatic institution is entirely independent of any particular day, set apart as holy; that the stress of the law lies on the proportion of time between the working days and the day of rest; that the Fourth Commandment does not determine which day of the week we should keep as a Sabbath, but only that we should keep every seventh day, or one day after six of labor; that the words of the commandment no way determine where these six days should begin, nor where the rest of the Sabbath should fall; that the obligation to keep holy a seventh part of time, or one day in seven, is perpetual and universal; that the holy rest itself is one thing, the particular day on which we are required to rest quite another. Hence, it is contended that, whatever defect there may be in the argument for the first day of the week in particular, it can in no way affect the general question, as the sabbatic institution would still remain.

Granting (for the argument's sake) that the institution and the day are quite distinct from each other, it can not be admitted that this distinction makes the one *independent* of the other; for the day holds such an important relation to the institution as to be essential to its integrity. A screw or a bolt is a distinct thing by itself; yet in a steam-engine, or in a road-carriage, it is a very important part of the structure, and holds such a relation to it that, if taken away or lost, the structure falls to pieces. So with the sabbatic institution and the day to be set apart for rest ; the day is so necessary to the institution, that without it the institution has nothing but an ideal existence. Its real or actual existence is gone the moment the sacredness of the day is gone.

But the notion that the sabbatic institution was ordained before the day of rest was designated, is a sheer fallacy : there is nothing in the Bible to support it. The inspired account is simply this : that the Creator, having rested on a certain day, from all his work, blessed and sanctified *that* DAY.* The fourth commandment is simply an injunction to remember *that* DAY, and to keep IT holy.†
Careful examination of these two pas-

* Gen. 2 : 2, 3. † Exod. 20 : 8-11.

sages shows that every thing predicated concerning the Sabbath has reference to the *day*, and not to the institution apart from the day. The Creator's rest is represented as taking effect on a certain *day;* that day he blessed and sanctified; that *day* we are required to remember and keep holy; in that *day* we are forbidden to do any work. There is no account of an institution previous to a day. On the contrary, the Creator sanctified the *day* on which he rested, and the sabbatic institution is the result growing out of it.

Now, if our Sunday sabbatarians will but show that the day whose observance they are trying to promote is *the* day upon which the Creator rested from his work; that it is *the* day which he then sanctified and blessed; that it is *the* day which we are commanded to remember and keep holy; they will have removed—not *every* difficulty, to be sure, but—a very great obstacle to its being regarded as holy to the Lord.

They owe it to themselves and the cause they advocate to do this. For notwithstanding their pretense that, whatever defect there may be in the argument for the first day of the week, the general question is not at all affected by it, they always insist upon the keeping holy of this day, in particular; they insist upon nothing else. They always speak of this day, and urge it upon the regard of others, as if it were the divinely appointed day. It is not the general question, about which they are so anxious; it is the sanctification of the *Sunday*, that they are laboring for. They are not so wanting in wit as to write books, and get up Conventions, and send out an army of agents, and all for nothing but the general question— the sanctification of *one day in seven*. They have an object before them—a defi-

nite one ; and that is to make every body
think that the first day of the week is holy
time.   They will succeed in this, when they
show that it is *the* day, concerning which
the Fourth Commandment says, ' Remember to keep it holy.'

Whether they are able to show this, is
not now the question : but it is plain that
the solicitude they feel, and the zeal they
manifest, go upon the supposition that
the *day* of the Sabbath is particularly specified somewhere in the word of God ; that
if not thus specified in the Fourth Commandment—the law of the Sabbath—it
is clearly specified in some other part
of Scripture, and *so* clearly as to leave
no room for mistake.   For though they
sometimes tell us that the Decalogue
makes no designation of the day ; that it
fixes only the proportion of time, every
seventh day, for devotional rest, but leaves
the date of the reckoning, and of course

the day itself, to be determined by positive law, or some other means ; they are, nevertheless, quite sure that the day is determined somewhere in the word of God, and that Sunday, or the first day of the week, is the day.

But whether this detaching of the day to be sanctified from the law commanding its sanctification is a likely way to promote obedience to the institution, and worthy of Infinite Wisdom to adopt, let the candid judge.

But we do not claim that the defect of the argument for the holiness of the first day of the week is the *only* obstacle to be overcome. On the contrary, though Christians were unanimous in observing the day for which they might plead a " thus saith the Lord," unrenewed men would still make opposition ; and the probability is, that their opposition would be more decided than their opposition to other duties of the

Moral Law. For Sabbath-keeping is not merely a well-bred concession to good morals; it is in reality nothing less than a *profession of religion.* It is an act, in which one solemnly declares allegiance to the God that made " heaven and earth, the sea and all that in them is;" a mode in which he avows a hearty consecration to the system of religion set forth in the Moral Law. In this it is like all other positive institutions, which are simply so many forms, under which the worshipers consecrate themselves to the particular system of religion, of which such institutions are a part.*

---

* The positive institutions of Baptism and the Lord's Supper are the divinely appointed forms under which believers consecrate themselves to and profess the Christian religion. Circumcision, the Passover, and other positive institutions of the Old Covenant, were forms, under which the Israelites were dedicated to the religion of Judaism. The Bible contains three distinct systems of religion, to each of which is appropriated one or more positive institutions. These systems are the Moral Law, Judaism, and Christianity. The first exhibits God as the Creator of all things; the second exhibits him as the tutelary Deity of a chosen nation; the third exhibits him as the Saviour of mankind. The strangest of all strange things is that there should be any misconceiving to which of these systems the Sabbath properly belongs.

Now, there are multitudes of men who respect morality, but hate religion. Thou shalt not kill, Thou shalt not steal, Thou shalt not commit adultery, Honor thy father and mother; all these have they kept from their youth up, and they mean to keep them to their dying day. They concede so much to the cause of morality. But they practice these moral duties, not because they constitute a system of religion which God commands, but because they agree with their own sense of what is fit and becoming. Higher than this they can not rise. If you add to these duties that of keeping the Sabbath holy, you put them at once upon a profession of allegiance to the great God who made them, whom they love not, and against whom their carnal heart rises in enmity. They will not stoop to it. In morality (so called) they glory; of religion they are ashamed.

For this reason, it is a great mistake to

suppose that true Sabbath-keeping can ever become popular with the worldly part of mankind. The attempt to make the desecration of the Sabbath odious, like other sins against the Moral Law, is simply visionary; it can not be done. Ministers may denounce it as a very wicked thing; they may represent it as the high road to the prison and the gallows; they may put Sabbath-breakers in the same category with robbers and murderers, and thus try to make their conduct hateful to the lovers of good order; but the attempt will ever be a failure. Men will not be driven into what they can not help regarding as, in some sense, a profession of religion. Nor does conscience reproach them for such refusal. For though they should become convinced that the Moral Law is a system of religion commanded by the Creator, and feel that they are guilty for not keeping it on this ground, they judge that it would be only hy-

pocrisy to make such a *profession* of this religion as Sabbath-keeping implies. It will
answer well enough for those who sincerely
worship God to do so, they say ; but that we
who never worship him should be required
to acknowledge him by keeping the Sabbath, is requiring us to profess what we do
not feel, and is very much like saying that a
person should be baptized although he does
not believe in Christianity.

This view suggests an additional reason
why the Sunday observance meets with so
much opposition from worldly men. For
though the keeping. of the first day of the
week holy is not the divinely appointed
method of professing the religion of the
Moral Law, its advocates claim thus much
for it, and even more. They make it a
memorial of Christ's resurrection, and so
constitute it a symbol of the Christian faith.
Thus, by representing it at one time as an
important part of the Moral Law, and

at another as a Gospel institution — the
Christian Sabbath — and pressing their
views with great earnestness and much
parade of learning, they cause some to
think that it is really of divine appointment. But by creating this impression,
they have unwittingly increased the difficulty of securing for it a popular observance, inasmuch as they have now
brought the institution into a shape which
makes it, more than it was before, the symbol of a religious profession.

Unconverted men are not willing to be
thought religious. They are not unwilling
to be thought moral; but their morality is
of a kind that has no God in it. The *social*
duties of the Decalogue are their admira-
tion; but the Decalogue as a system of
religion is their detestation.

True Sabbath keeping, therefore—such
Sabbath keeping as expresses homage to
the Creator—can make progress in the

world, only as pure and undefiled religion prevails. When the revolted creature is, by the power of the Gospel, brought to acknowledge and sincerely worship the God who made heaven and earth, the sea and all that in them is, then, and not till then, will he truly sabbatize.

There is still another reason why the cause of Sabbath reform moves so heavily. It is advocated upon grounds quite too low. The fashion is, and has been for some time, to urge the physical and intellectual adaptations of a day of rest, its economical bearings, its connection with personal respectability and happiness, its domestic and national benefits—in a word, its conduciveness to man's well-being here in this world, as the prominent and weighty reasons for its observance. Gilfillan has gone into this largely. In fact, it seems to be the staple of his argument.

Such considerations, it is true, are well

adapted to influence worldly men. They can
feel the force of an argument which appeals
to their love of property, of honor, of ease
and respectability. Prove to them that life
will be prolonged by resting from toil one
day in seven; that their fields will yield
better and their crops be more secure; that
their beasts of burden will do more work,
their servants labor with better heart, and
the whole business of life be more thriftily
conducted; and they will at once avail
themselves of the advantages thus pro-
mised. Yet what is it, after all, that moves
them but pure selfishness?

To rest the plea for a divine institution
on such grounds is such a lowering of its
dignity, that it may well be questioned
whether the blessing of God—without
which Paul plants and Apollos waters in
vain—can attend it. Not but what it is
true that these temporal advantages, to a
certain extent, do flow from a day of rest;

but it is a truth of small importance, compared with the higher and holier considerations on which the Fourth Commandment
claims obedience, and ought never to be
emphasized beyond its real significance.

What would be thought of the Christian
minister, who should urge men to embrace
the Gospel, chiefly on the ground that
"godliness has promise of the life that now
is"? Would he not be justly chargeable
with losing sight of the great end for which
Christ commanded the Gospel to be
preached? Would he not lessen the dignity of his subject? Would he succeed in
winning souls? Would the Holy Spirit
honor such preaching? Yet it were about
as wise thus to commend the Gospel to the
unconverted,—for they could feel the force
of such arguments,—as to urge Sabbath
observance on the ground of its temporal
advantages. And it is a question for both
Mr. Gilfillan, and all others who write in

like strain, to consider, whether they have not pressed this argument for a day of rest far beyond its just bounds, thereby degrading the subject, and offending Him whose blessing is necessary to the success of all endeavors to recover sinners from the error of their ways.

Those who take their day of rest directly from the Fourth Commandment, have no hesitation in resting the obligation to keep it upon the reason which is given in the commandment itself. They find there no other reason but this : "*for in six days the Lord made heaven and earth, the sea and all that in them is, and rested the seventh day. Wherefore the Lord blessed the Sabbath-day, and hallowed it.*" Which shows that God made the institution a memorial of his power, wisdom, and goodness, as displayed in the work of creation. He ordained it for an everlasting testimony against Atheism and Idolatry ; a testimony that the world did not spring into existence by *chance*, or some *fortuitous concurrence of atoms*, but was the product of Infinite Power; that it was not left in chaotic confusion—"without form and void"—nor left to work its way blindly out of that confusion; but that His own hand fashioned every thing in beauteous order, and made all things "very good;" that in all this work he wrought alone, not calling to his aid any such gods as the heathen worship, his own right hand laying the foundation of the earth, and spanning the heavens, and his own voice calling forth all their host.

This was the ground upon which the Sabbath was commanded to Israel. It was "*a sign*" between Jehovah and them. A "sign" of what? Why, that the God "who sanctified them," the God they had undertaken to worship, was not such a being as the heathen worshiped, but was the true Creator of all things.*

* See Exod. 31 : 13, 17; also Ezek. 20 : 12, 20, with context.

Accordingly, when *we*, the observers of the *seventh* day, exhort men to keep the Sabbath, we put it at once upon this ground. We tell them that they are God's creatures, gifted with exalted powers, and capable of knowing, loving, and serving him that made them ; that they are held in being' by his power; that they ought to acknowledge him, and feel their accountability to him, not living as if they had made themselves and were independent of his care, nor setting up such objects of worship as they do who are ignorant of the Creator. We tell them that the Sabbath is designed to keep them in mind of these obligations ; for it points directly to that creative work in which they originate ; that it is thus an institution, through and by which they are to religiously acknowledge him in whom they live and move and have their being, and by which to testify against the lies which would dethrone him from the world which he made. In short, we tell them that the Sabbath is "a sign," that the God who sanctifies them, and calls them to worship him, is the Creator of all worlds ; and we urge them to keep it *on this account.* For is he the God of the Jews only? Is he not of the Gentiles also? (Rom. 3 : 29.) *

Thus we put the Sabbath at once upon high and holy ground. We take it just as God gives it to us : and just as he gives it to us, we enjoin it upon others, not troubling ourselves with the apprehension that, because they are dead in trespasses

---

* That the Sabbath was "a sign" between God and the Israelites, is converted by some into an argument that it was peculiar to the chosen nation, continuing only during the Mosaic dispensation. But of what was it a sign? "That ye may know that I am the Lord that doth sanctify you." And is it not a sign of the same thing to all others who worship Israel's God? Does it not signify to us, Gentiles, that He who has sanctified us (called us into his service) is the Lord Jehovah—the same God that the Israelites worshiped? The Sabbath was "a sign" that the God who "sanctified" the children of Israel was not such a God as the heathen worshiped, but the Creator, who in six days made heaven and earth, and on the seventh day rested and was refreshed. Is it not a sign of the same thing to us? (See Exod. 31 : 13-17, and compare Ezek. 20 : 12, 20.)

and sins, they will not appreciate the argument. We leave that with God, assured that he has not called us to employ reasoning seasoned to the taste of carnal men. We believe that all the physical, intellectual, and temporal advantages, which are claimed as resulting from the keeping of Sunday, would be as surely secured by the observance of the day of the command- ment. But though these additional advan- tages would be reasons for greater thank- fulness on the part of those who have already come into possession of the holy rest, it is not on such grounds that we urge men to observe it. We urge them to keep the Sabbath, even though they should be *impoverished* by doing so. We plead for it as the memorial of God's rest at the close of creation. We urge it as the di- vinely appointed observance, through which the creature man is to make a solemn ex-

pression of his obligation to, and depen-
dence on, the Author of his being.

Is it because the Sunday observance has
no such ground to stand upon, that its advocates are unwilling to rest the argument
here? Do they see that the first day of the
week is not a suitable time for commemora-
ting a rest which occurred on the seventh?
Do they see that an observance, held on the
weekly return of the day when God *began*
his work, is not suited for the commemoration of a rest entered upon after his
work was *finished.* Do they thus see and
feel, that their Sunday celebration is no
suitable memorial of creation completed,
beautified, gloriously furnished, and all
"very good"? And is it for this reason,
that they drop all allusion to the creation,
after barely stating it, and begin to talk of
the Redemption work of Christ as the foundation of their festival; and then, as if this
were too much above the appreciation of

carnal men, turn to the consideration of the temporal benefits of the institution ? These are questions for themselves to ponder, but we certainly think they are pertinent to the subject.

The argument for a hebdomadal rest from its physical and temporal benefits is not altogether satisfactory. Many honest minds fail to see its conclusiveness. The argument alleges that "a period of rest, after six days' continued toil, is indispensable to the laborer; without this gracious interval, his strength and vigor prematurely decay. Nor is this interval of repose, as a law of our physical nature, less necessary to intellectual occupations. The mind must be statedly unladen of its cares, as the body of its burdens, or a similar penalty must be endured." *

"The observance of the Sabbath is required by a *natural law*; and were man nothing more than an animal, and were his existence to be confined to this world, it would be for his interest to observe the Sabbath. Should all the business which is

* *Address of the Baltimore National Sabbath Convention*, 1844.

not required by the appropriate duties of
the Sabbath be confined to six days' in a
week, . . . both man and beast might enjoy higher health, obtain longer life, and do
more work, and in a better manner, than
by the secular employment of the whole
seven." *

Dr. Humphrey cites the following case :
" A contractor went on to the West, with his
hired men and teams, to make a turnpike
road. At first, he paid no regard to the
Sabbath, but continued his work as on
other days. He soon found, however, that
the ordinances of nature, no less than the
moral law, were against him. His laborers
became sickly, his teams grew poor and
feeble ; and being fully convinced that more
was lost than gained by working on the
Lord's Day, he desisted. So true is it, that
the Sabbath-day laborer, like the glutton
and the drunkard, undermines his health,

* *Permanent Sabbath Documents*, p. 60.

and prematurely hastens the infirmities of age and his exit from this world." *

"Man was created for six days' work, not for seven ; his faculties can not bear an unremitted strain. . . . The utmost producive labor of man is in the proportion of rest and exertion, ordained by his merciful Creator. The best prevention of disease is in the same provision. The prolongation of human life depends on the like alternation of toil and repose." †

"An occasional season of rest beyond that of night is of advantage to our physical nature, adjusting the measure of labor to the laborer's 'strength, and lightening its pressure by inspiring cheerfulness and hope ; and to this extent the Sabbath, while it makes provision for the inferior animals according to their more limited

---

* *Wilson on the Lord's Day.* Serm. vi.
† *Pres. Humphrey on the Sabbath Cuestion,* v. sect. 5.

wants, is adapted to the necessities and to
the well-being of man."

"Manual laborers will be found nearly
unanimous in the conviction that continuous
toil is destructive to health ; and we have
seen upward of one thousand of them pub-
lishing to the world their persuasion that a
weekly day of exemption from toil, and yet
spent not in total inaction or amusement
but in the duties of piety and benevolence
is indispensable to their physical welfare,
and even to the preservation of life. One
of them remarks, that ' on more than one
occasion he has found that continued appli-
cation to labor during six days in the busy
season, and consequent long hours, was
more than his constitution would bear, and
that if he had attempted to dispense with
the relaxation of the Sabbath, he should
long since, he firmly believed, have retired
to the rest and silence of the grave.' " *

* *Gilfillan,* pp. 178, 181.

In reference to the view thus presented we remark that, supposing the Sabbath to be a divine institution, and of perpetual and universal obligation, the idea that our physical nature is adjusted to such a distribution of time has a strong presumption in its favor. For there is doubtless a perfect harmony between the works of God and his laws. We who maintain the perpetuity of the sabbatic institution have, therefore, no interest in denying this view. But there is another class of persons, neither small nor despicable, who maintain, (and are doubtless honest in maintaining,) that the Sabbath was a purely Jewish institution, and has no binding force under the Gospel. And what is such an argument to them? They find a sufficient answer to it in saying that, if men were not overworked on the six days, they would not need the seventh as a day of rest. Their views may be stated as follows : ' That it is true in general that the physical nature of man is benefited by rest. ing one day in seven, will not be denied. There is a maximum to the labor of men and animals, as well as of inanimate machines, which can not be exceeded without injury. If there is a certain amount of labor to be performed in a month, a year, or any other given period, this amount will be accomplished with much less injury to the man, animal, or machine, by a regular division of it, than in any other way. As a relief from ex-cessive toil, a rest of one day in seven is necessary to the laborer. But would he need it, if his toil were not too great on the other six ?   Is it not from causes, which in themselves are violations of the laws of nature, that it becomes necessary ? If, because he works ten hours a day, he needs one day in seven for rest, would he need it if he worked but eight hours ?

Such, substantially, is the answer of anti-sabbatarians, nor is it easy to show its fallacy.

In Gilfillan, as in most other modern publications, a large space is devoted to this point, the object being to show that the Sabbath has its foundation in our nature. But the argument must ever seem worthless to those who have been trained in a theological system· denying the perpetuity of the Sabbath under the Gospel. It is adapted only to those who are otherwise well convinced that the Sabbath is a divine institution, but refuse to act in accordance with their convictions. If the Sabbath is indeed a divine institution, binding alike on Gentiles and Jews and of force under the Gospel, then it is a reasonable supposition that its rest of one whole day in seven will better conduce to the restoration of wasted strength, whether of body or mind, and to the utmost prolongation of life, than any considerable amount of rest every day. But it is not likely that statistics have been compiled with such accuracy as to afford reliable data for a decision of this mooted question. The case of the contractor who went West, cited by President Humphrey, and quoted again by Gilfillan, was doubtless one where the laborers and teams was driven to a full day's work every day. All the cases cited in *Permanent Sabbath Documents* (where there is quite a list of them) must be put in the same category. But no pains were ever taken (we think) to collect statistics on the other side of the question, and then to make the comparison. It has never yet been conclusively shown that those who regard all days alike, and take plenty of time for rest every day, do not live to old age, nor enjoy the comforts of life while they do live. And until this is shown, it is very poor logic to infer the necessity of a Sabbath from instances of those who were, in all probability, subjected to excessive toil.

But conceding the utmost to this method of argument, what does it prove for the first day of the week? Nothing whatever. It would prove just as much for any other day of the seven, that might be devoted to rest, as it does for the Sunday. But this flaw in the argument is repaired by the discovery that the providential government of the world is administered altogether in the interest of Sunday. Accordingly besides these examples of persons exhausting the powers of life by incessant toil on all days of the week, others are adduced of persons who, disregarding the popular day of rest, are smitten with the judgments of heaven! One man harvests his grain on Sunday, and his barn is struck by lightning and the grain consumed. A merchant makes out an invoice of goods on Sunday to send out by steamer on Monday, and upon those goods loses ten thousand dollars. Vessels leave port on Sunday, and are wrecked, involving great loss of life and property. A man travels on a steamboat, on the Ohio River, and one of his sweet little children falls overboard and is drowned. Another makes money rapidly for a series of years by working on Sunday, and at last all his property comes under the sheriff's hammer, and he dies—a poor man. And many other instances of a similar character are related.

Now, these facts, for aught we know, may have occurred just as related; but to the interpretation put upon them we demur. If a calamity following an act determines the act to have been one of rebellion against God, what shall we say of those who had trial of cruel mockings and scourgings, yea, moreover of bonds and imprisonment; who were stoned, sawn asunder, slain with the sword, wandered about in sheepskins and goatskins, destitute, afflicted, tormented? If worldly prosperity is a sign of God's approbation, then what shall we say of those who are not in trouble as other men, neither are they plagued like other men; whose eyes stand out with fatness and they have more than heart could wish? Do calamities never overtake the righteous? Does prosperity never come upon the wicked? In the final summing up of all things at the great Judgment Day, no doubt, it will be well with the righteous and ill with the wicked; but the veriest tyro in the school of Christ knows, or ought to know, that a person's earthly condition is no certain index of his standing in the sight of God.

We do not mean to intimate that calamities such as are here referred to come without cause, or that they are not ordered and directed by God. But God has his own reasons for sending them, and he has not made it our province to say what those reasons are. Whenever we undertake to determine matters so intricately wrapped in mystery, we are certain to show how little is our knowledge of the counsels of Heaven. The facts referred to are facts to be studied ; their meaning carefully and solemnly pondered. But it could be wished that the attempts to interpret them in the interest of a day, the divine authority of which is yet far from undisputed, were made with a little more modesty. To the authors of such attempts we commend a passage in the life of the Apostle Paul.*

* See Acts 28 : 3-6.

Dismissing this argument, therefore, as well as all others which rest the Sabbath on doubtful grounds, and confining ourselves to the clearer teachings of truth, we remark that the Sabbath is a strictly *commemorative* institution. It was designed to serve, not only under the Law, but under the Gospel, and through all ages to the end of time, as a *memorial celebration* of a completed, gloriously wrought, and " very good " creation. Thus it was made a standing testimony against *Atheism* and *Idolatry*— against the proneness of men to say on the one hand that there is no God, and on the other that there are many gods. And when we remember that these are the two bitter roots from which have grown all the varieties of sin that have prevailed among men—enmity against God developing itself either in the abominations of idolatry, or (where the abundance of light forbids such grossness) in rejecting the idea of a Being who governs the world and holds his creatures accountable — it will be seen that such a testimony was and is still needed. For atheism is still in the world. Not the blank atheism of former days ; that has given place to more elaborate and refined ways of ignoring the great First Cause ; but atheism nevertheless, which under various names and guises is spreading its mischief far and wide. As for idolatry, it still holds the greater part of mankind in its bondage ; though instead of being more refined than at first, it has grown more and more corrupt. The original purer forms of it, such as the worship of the heavenly luminaries, have degenerated into baser systems. But they all rob the Creator of his glory, and keep out of view the fact that his own unaided hand made heaven and earth, the sea and all that in them is.

We urge the observance of the Sabbath, therefore, not because, like the other duties of the Moral Law, it is obviously founded in nature ; not because of its conduciveness to health, long life, prosperity in business, worldly comfort ; nor principally because of its conduciveness to good morals. But we urge it as a grand *celebration*, pointing to the great First Cause of all things, rebuking the atheism and idolatry of those who know not God, testifying against the impiety, profaneness, and vice, which are the fruits of such ignorance, and declaratory of the gladness which the works of God are fitted to inspire.*

We say a *celebration:* and the idea suggested by the term must be carefully considered, if we would understand the subject; for it is through inattention to this point that much confusion arises. Overlooking this idea, and regarding the Sab-

* Ps. 92 : 4

bath as only a season for resting wearied
nature and obtaining religious instruction,
it is difficult to see why one day will not
answer as well as another. And because
all the purposes of a Sabbath as thus defin-
ed seem to be answered by one day as well
as another, it is thought by some that a
wise lawgiver would not enjoin any particular day ; hence the conclusion that He
has not, and that the Fourth Commandment
does not mean any day in particular, but
only one day in seven, or the seventh after
six days of labor. But this error finds its
correction in the fact that the Sabbath is a
divinely appointed *celebration.*

Now, a celebration always has reference
to some particular *fact* or *event*, the memory
of which it seeks to perpetuate. The particular fact which the Sabbath celebration
refers to is the *rest* into which the Creator
entered on the last day of the first week of
time ; his work, which had occupied the

previous six days, being then finished. The law of the institution makes this perfectly clear. What does it command us to do? To keep holy the seventh day. *Why* are we commanded to keep the seventh day rather than any other? Because˙ that is *the* day which the Creator blessed and hallowed. Why did he bless and hallow *that* day? Because that in it he rested from all his work. Now, the day of the Creator's rest was most unquestionably the *last* day of the first week of time.* The day, therefore, which he blessed and sanctified or hallowed, and commands to be kept holy in its weekly returns, is the *last* or *seventh* day of the week. The commandment enjoins no other, nor will the reason for the observance apply to any other day.

It is amusing to witness the triumphant air with which some challenge us to show that the Sabbath law requires any thing

* See Gen. 2 : 2, 3.

more than the observance of one day in seven as a day of rest. A writer in one of our ablest religious papers talks in this style :

"The original command does not, as is commonly assumed, set apart a *particular day of the week* as holy to the Lord. It only hallows and sanctifies the seventh day, that is, as explained in the command itself, the day that follows six days of labor. The Fourth Commandment is just as literally obeyed by the Christian who hallows the first day of the week, as it is by the Jew who hallows the seventh day of the week. The question has been made to appear more formidable than it really is, and an unjust burden of proof has been thrown upon the observers of the first day of the week, by a groundless assumption at the outset. We have no right to add to the words of God, by inserting "of the week" after the word "day" in the Fourth Commandment."

To this our reply is very simple. The *words* " of the week" are not in the commandment ; nobody pretends that they are ; nobody wants them there. If they were there, no doubt the same perverseness that now tries to explain away the evident meaning of the commandment would find some way of making the week begin on Monday instead of Sunday. It is sufficient that the *idea* of the seventh day of the week is in the commandment.; and that it is we have clearly shown above.

Now, if the Sabbath was designed to be a weekly celebration of the Creator's rest, what propriety or fitness is there in holding this celebration on any other than the seventh day of the week? Do we celebrate American Independence on any other day of July but the *Fourth?* Is not Jackson's victory at New-Orleans always celebrated on the *eighth* of January? Is not Washington's Birthday celebrated on the *twenty-*

second of February? Is any celebration
whatever held on any but the annual,
monthly, or weekly return of the day on
which the event which is the foundation of
it took place?

The transfer of the Sabbath from the
seventh to the first day of the week is
therefore the destruction of the institution.
It is no longer a celebration of the Creator's
rest.   It no longer commemorates a finished
creation.   All of creation that it can possibly commemorate is what was brought into
being on the first day.   It is consequently
no longer a full testimony against atheism
and idolatry.   Hence, the observers of the
first day of the week touch this point very
cautiously.   Yet, as if to apologize for the
violence done to the original institution,
they eagerly claim for their practice that it
is a *celebration* of a not less, and even greater, event than the creation of the world.
The merits of this pretense will be examin-

ed hereafter. At present we only remark that, if it is a celebration of another and different event, it is cêrtainly another and different institution, and no logic can make it the same as that which is enjoined in the Fourth Commandment. Nevertheless, its advocates claim that it is the same!

The importance of commemorative institutions is not always understood. Because Christianity seems to undervalue and even to speak disparagingly of Jewish ordinances, it is thought by some that the observance of days clashes with the spirituality of the truth as it is in Jesus. With respect to the *typical* institutions of the Law, this idea is correct, but commemorative institutions stand upon a different footing. A commemorative institution is of the nature of a *monument* erected to perpetuate the memory of some important event, and its importance lies in the irrefragable proof which it furnishes that the event did actually take place. Wherever we see a monument, we know that it testifies to some important fact, and to learn what that fact is, we examine the inscription. Having read it, we feel no misgiving concerning the actuality of the fact; for we know that a monument testifying to a falsehood would not be allowed to stand. The boys of the street would soon tear it down, and the honest, truth-loving common people would sustain them in the act. Now, the Sabbath is a monument which has been set up as a memorial of creation, and upon it is this inscription, which God wrote with his own finger: that having created heaven, earth, and sea, and all that in them is, in six days, he rested the seventh day, and therefore blessed the seventh day, and sanctified it, constituting it the day of rest for man.

Who then shall undertake to destroy, alter, or change this inscription? Yet our

* See Mark 2 : 27.

Sunday brethren (we grieve to say it) have undertaken this sacrilegious act. They have sought to alter the inscription so as to make it testify to another and different fact. What is worse, they pretend that Christ and his Apostles took the lead in this matter. No, brethren, Christ never undertook to mutilate a monument which his Father had built. He did not go about to erase from its tablet the testimony which it bore against atheism and idolatry, that he might put in its place a testimony to his own proper work. He never thought of having Redemption commemorated at such an expense. Not Christ, but *Anti-Christ* was the originator of this movement, even that Wicked One concerning whom it was said, " He shall think to change times and laws." * The Sabbath-day, which from the beginning was a sacred day, this Anti-Christ has changed into a working day, so that it has become **the** busiest day of the week ; and the Sunday, which had always before been a working day,* he has changed into a sacred day.

Like most writers of the Puritan creed, Gilfillan holds that the Sabbath law requires merely the sanctification of one day in seven, and not of the seventh day of the week. Precisely which day of the seven is to be sanctified must be determined, therefore, not by the law of the institution, but by some other indication of the divine will in the matter. The resurrection of Christ has determined it to the first day of the week for the Christian Dispensation, that event having occurred on that day, as is generally supposed. Before the resurrection of Christ, it was the seventh or last day of the week which was to be kept sacred ; though how it was so determined, aside from the law of the institution, this writer has not informed us. True, Sabbata-

* Ezek. 46 : 1.

rians suppose that the law of the institution *always* determines the day ; that it determined it to the seventh day of the week under the Old Dispensation, and that it still so determines under the Christian economy. If the law of the institution does not now determine the day, it never did.

But the advocates of Sunday observance are not agreed among themselves as to the true construction of the law. President Humphrey declares, without hesitation, that the law commands the observance of the seventh day of the week.

The point is settled in these express words : " And on the *seventh* day God ended his work which he had made ; and he rested on the *seventh* day from all his work which he had made. And God blessed the *seventh* day, and sanctified it." The same day is specified in the confirmation or reënactment of the Sabbath at Mount Sinai.

'Six days shalt thou labor, and do all thy work ; but the *seventh* is the Sabbath of the Lord thy God.' Indeed, wherever the weekly Sabbath is mentioned in the Old Testament, the *seventh* day of the week is intended."

Other writers, however, contend that "the Decalogue knows nothing of Saturday. It makes no designation of the day. It fixes only the proportion of time, every seventh for devotional rest, but leaves the date of the reckoning, and of course the day itself, to be determined by positive law, or some other means. For the Jews this had been previously determined by the miracle of the Manna." *

What we have to say is that, if this last is the true construction of the Sabbath law, it took the religious world a great while to find it out. From the creation to the resur-

* J. N. Brown, Discussion with W. B. Taylor.

rection of Christ, God's people seem never to have thought of such a construction. They all, without exception, seem to have regarded the day of the Sabbath as fixed by the law of the institution.* Nor is there under the new dispensation the least trace of any such construction till near the close of the 16th century. The Sunday festival, it is true, had been promoted to honor long before this, but nobody pretended to find justification for it in the Fourth Commandment. During the dark ages, attempts were made to find a divine warrant for it, and to this end various impostures were practiced upon the people. Miracles, apparitions, supernatural documents, whatever tricks a cunning priesthood could devise, were employed to persuade the super-

---

* The clear-sightedness of our Baptist brethren, when the ordinance of baptism is under discussion, is remarkable. Go to the law of circumcision to determine the subjects of baptism ! No, indeed : it is the law of the institution which determines the subjects of the ordinance. We wish they were equally discerning in reference to the Sabbath.

stitious people that the Sunday festival had been ratified in heaven.* But that it was

---

* " Henry II. entered on the government about the year :155. Of him it is reported that he had an apparition at Cardiff (in South-Wales) which, from St. Peter, charged him, that upon Sundays throughout the year, there should be no buying or selling, and no servile work done." (Mosen, p. 283 ; Heylyn, part 2, chap. 7, sec. 6.)

" In the very entrance of the thirteenth age, Fulco, a French priest and a notable hypocrite, lighted upon a new Sabbatarian fancy, which one of his associates, Eustachius, abbot of Flay, in Normandy, was sent to scatter here in England ; but finding opposition to his doctrines, he went back again. The next year after, being 1202, he comes better fortified, preaching from town to town and from place to place, that no man should market on the Lord's day. Now for the easier bringing of the people to obey their dictates, they had to show a warrant sent from God himself, as they gave it out. The title was this :

" ' A HOLY MANDATE, touching the Lord's day, which came down from heaven unto Jerusalem, found on St. Simeon's altar in Golgotha, where Christ was crucified for the sins of all the world, which lying there three days and three nights, struck with such terror all that saw it, that, falling on the ground, they besought God's mercy. At last the patriarch and Akarias, the archbishop, (of I know not whence,) ventured to take into their hands that dreadful letter, which was written thus. Now wipe your eyes and look awhile on the contents :

" ' I am the Lord who commanded you to keep the Lord's day, and you have not kept it, neither repented of your sins ; I caused repentance to be preached unto you, and you believed not ; then I sent the pagans among you, who spilt your blood on the earth, and yet you believed not ; and because you did not observe the Lord's holy day, I punished you awhile with famine, but in a short time I gave you fullness of bread, and then you behaved yourselves worse than before. I again charge you that from the ninth hour [that is, three o'clock p. m.] on Saturday, until sunrising on the Monday, no man may presume to do any work, but what is good, or if he do, let him repent for the same. Verily I say unto you, and swear by my seat and throne, and by the cherubim which surround it, that if you do not hearken to this my mandate, I will send no other letter unto you, but will open the heavens and sanctioned by Scripture—the revealed law of God—nobody ever thought of pretending.

rain upon you stones, wood, and scalding water by night, so that none shall be able to provide against them. I say ye shall die the death for the Lord's day, and other festivals of my saints which ye have not kept ; and I will send among you beasts with the heads of lions, and the hair of women, and the tails of camels, which being very hungry shall devour your flesh. And you shall desire to flee to the sepulchres of the dead, and hide you for fear of those beasts. And I will take the light of the sun from your eyes, and send such darkness that not being able to see, you shall destroy each other. And I will turn my face away and not in the least pity you. I will burn your bodies and hearts of all them who do not keep the Lord's day. Hear then my words and do not perish for neglecting this day. I swear to you by my right hand, that if you do not observe the Lord's day, and festivals of my saints, I will send pagan nations to destroy you.'" (Heylyn's Hist. Sab. part 2, chap. 7, sect. 6. Moren, pp. 288–290.)

One is sometimes ready to ask whether our modern advocates of the Sunday observance ever had their attention directed to these facts. For it seems almost incredible that honest, God-fearing men, in the face of such facts, would continue to assert, as they do, that the observance has always been regarded as a fulfillment of the Sabbath law. But whatever may be said of some others, Gilfillan can not plead ignorance in the matter. He cites the very cases which we have now cited, (p. 399 of his work,) but instead of being ashamed of and denouncing them as contrivances of " that wicked," whose coming is after the working of Satan, he apologizes for them, varnishing them over by saying that the resort to them " was significant of the importance supposed to belong to it," (the Sunday festival ;) thus insinuating that it was zeal for the *Sabbath* which was at the bottom of such exceptionable measures, whereas in fact it was only zeal for the authority of the Church. The apparition seen by Henry II. "has a meaning and use to the extent of indicating the opinion that the day was the charge of Heaven, and that its sacred observance was connected with human prosperity and happiness." He thinks " the same lesson is taught by the case of Eustachius,

The light of the Reformation destroyed the support which the Sunday festival had obtained from these impostures, and left it nothing to stand upon but the decrees of councils, the edicts of kings and emperors, and the mandates of the Pope. Other festivals of the Church, however, stood upon the same authority; Christmas, Easter, the Ascension, Whitsunday, Epiphany, and many of less note. All these were maintained by the Church of England. But the Puritans, between whom and the Episcopalians the controversy reached its greatest height in the 16th century, were not content to rest their practice upon such authority, but contended earnestly that the only rule of faith for Christians was the Bible.

Abbot de Flay." Verily, he might make the same plea in behalf of all the idolatrous festivals of the Church of Rome. In fact, he does; only instead of finding them "significant of the importance supposed to belong to" those festivals particularly, he thinks that they "had their origin in the recognized authority and felt benefit of the only true holy day." But one that could find in such things proof of the divine appointment of the.Sunday observance, could find it anywhere.

Yet as they held fast to the Sunday, and rejected all the other festivals, they were driven to the alternative of either giving it up entirely or of defending its observance by the Bible. A German writer of distinction thus states the issue:

"The opinion that the Sabbath was transferred to the Sunday was first broached in its perfect form, and with all its consequences, in the controversy which was carried on in England between the Episcopalians and Presbyterians. . . . . . . The Presbyterians were now in a position which compelled them either to give up the observance of the Sunday, or to maintain that a divine appointment from God separated it from the other festivals. . . . . . They therefore decided upon the latter." * A writer, the accuracy of whose statements has not been questioned by Gilfillan or any of his fellow laborers in the interest of

---

* Hengstenberg's Lord's Day, p. 66.

Sunday, gives the following exact account
of the matter:

"The true doctrine of the Christian Sabbath was first promulgated by an English
dissenter, the Rev. Nicholas Bound, D.D.,
of Norton, in the county of Suffolk. About
the year 1595, he published a famous book,
entitled 'Sabbathum Veteris et Novi Testa-
menti,' or The True Doctrine of the Sabbath. In this book he maintained 'that the
seventh part of our time ought to be devoted to God—that Christians are bound to
rest on the Lord's day as much as the Jews
were on the Mosaic Sabbath, the commandment about rest being moral and perpetual;
and that it was not lawful for persons to
follow their studies or worldly business on
that day, nor to use such pleasures and
recreations as are permitted on other days.'
This book spread with wonderful rapidity.
The doctrine which it propounded called
forth from many hearts a ready response,

and the result was a most pleasing reformation in many parts of the kingdom. 'It is
almost incredible,' says Fuller, 'how taking
this doctrine was, partly because of its own
purity, and partly for the eminent piety of
such persons as maintained it; so that the
Lord's day, especially in corporations, began to be precisely kept; people becoming a
law unto themselves, forbearing such sports
as yet by statute permitted; yea, many re-
joicing at their own restraint herein.' The
law of the Sabbath was indeed a religious
principle, after which the Christian church
had, for centuries, been darkly groping.
Pious men of every age had felt the necessity of divine authority for sanctifying the
day. Their conscience had been in advance of their reason. Practically they
had kept the Sabbath better than their
principles required.

"Public sentiment, however, was still un-
settled in regard to this new doctrine re-

specting the Sabbath, though a few at first violently opposed it. Learned men were very much divided in their judgments about these Sabbatarian doctrines; some embraced them as ancient truths consonant to Scripture, long disused and neglected, now seasonably revised for the increase of piety. Others conceived them grounded on a wrong bottom; but because they tended to the manifest advance of religion, it was a pity to oppose them; seeing none have just reason to complain, being deceived unto their own good. But a third sort flatly fell out with these propositions, as galling men's necks with a *Jewish yoke* against the liberty of Christians; that Christ, as Lord of the Sabbath, had removed the rigor thereof, and allowed men lawful recreations; *that this doctrine put an unequal lustre on the Sunday*, on set purpose to eclipse all other holy days, to the derogation of the authority of the church; that this strict observance was set up out of faction, to be a character of difference to brand all for libertines who did not entertain it. No open opposition, however, was at first manifested against the sentiments of Dr. Bound. No reply was attempted for several years.

"His work was soon followed by several other treatises in defense of the same sentiments. 'All the Puritans fell in with this doctrine, and distinguished themselves by spending that part of sacred time in public, family, and private devotion.' Even Dr. Heylin certified the triumphant spread of those puritanical sentiments respecting the Sabbath. . . . .

"'This doctrine,' he says, 'carrying such a fair show of piety, at least in the opinion of the common people, and such as did not examine the true grounds of it, induced many to embrace and defend it; and in a very little time it became the most bewitching error and the most popular infatuation that ever was embraced by the people of England.'"*

The reader will take particular notice, therefore, that the first attempt to construe the Fourth Commandment as requiring merely the observance of one day in seven was made less than three hundred years ago, and that Dr. Nicholas Bound was the originator of the idea. Before his time, nobody had doubted that the Commandment required the observance of the seventh day of the week.

This "one day in seven" theory is a great convenience to those who contend for a change of the Sabbath. Indeed, they could do nothing without it; for any one can see that, if the law of the Sabbath requires the observance of a particularly specified day, it is folly to talk of the perpetuity of the law and yet argue for a change too. If the law requires a particularly specified day, a re-

* Coleman's Ancient Christianity Exemplified, chap. 26, sec. 2.

fusal to keep that day is disobedience to the law. Of course, all Sunday sabbatarians stick to the theory of Dr. Bound. Anointed with this eye-salve, they clearly see that "a dispensation so important, and in some respects so new as ·that of Christianity, might be presumed to require, in adaptation to its own character and purposes, some alterations in the Sabbath. It might be expected, for example, that the work of redemption would have a prominent niche and statue in this monumental institute. The Scriptures had presented this work as one that should cast all preceding works into the shade. They had told us of a new creation more glorious than the old, and therefore more entitled to remembrance; of a redemption more precious far than the rescue from Egyptian thraldom, and therefore much more worthy to be immortalized. If the material creation merited a memorial, much more the moral; if the temporal deliverance of a single nation deserved to have an institution enacted in its honor, incalculably more the spiritual and eternal salvation of a multitude that no man can number." *

"There is another event of extensive and abiding importance—an event greater than the Creation, as it reveals more of the character of the Supreme Being, and secures a higher and more enduring, even an eternal happiness to man. Compared with Redemption, all other works are unworthy to 'come into mind.' To this completed work the Lord's Day has been indissolubly linked." †

So then, according to this author, the original design of the Sabbath—which was to commemorate a finished creation, and thus give testimony against Atheism and Idolatry—is to be lost sight of, "cast into the shade," that "a new creation, more glo-

---

* Gilfillan, pp. 301, 302.   † *Ibid.* p. 339.

rious than the old," may be had in remembrance.

Now, let us look this argument calmly in the face. It assumes that Redemption is "an event greater than the Creation." We shall not dispute it. But for the very reason that it is greater, we submit whether it can be commemorated by the observance of any day whatever. *Days* are measures of time which were established by the creation, all the days of the week growing out of that great work. Events of time, or transactions having their scope and range in this world, may well be commemorated by days set apart for the purpose. But a work which began in the counsels of eternity, whose bearing is upon man's eternal destiny, whose fruits and results are but imperfectly accomplished in time, their grand consummation being reserved for the heavenly state, is not commemorated by "days, months, and times, and years." Hence the Christian economy, *as such*, is entirely wanting in such appointments, though Judaism, whose domain is in this world, is well stocked with them.* Christianity has its commemorative institutions, it is true— Baptism and the Supper—the one being a memorial of the death of the Saviour, the other of his burial and resurrection ; but it is remarkable that in giving these memorials, our Saviour designated no *days* for their observance. Simply the facts are thought worthy of commemoration, and they are supposed to be suitably commemorated whenever the worshipers are in a state of readiness: the Lord's death, "as oft" as the church in an orderly way shall come together for the purpose ; his Resurrection, whenever one avowing himself a believer† shall say, 'What doth hinder me to be baptized ?'

---

* See Gal. 4 : 3, 9; Col. 2 : 8, 20; Heb. 9 : 1.
† Mark 16 : 16.

Now, whether this view is convincing to the reader or not, certain it is that Jesus Christ appointed no *day* on which to commemorate the work of Redemption, and in the absence of such appointment any reasoning concerning the necessity for such a day is being wise above what is written. Because God saw fit to appoint a Sabbath to commemorate creation, we can not hence infer the necessity for one to commemorate Redemption. Still less can we infer the discontinuance of that Sabbath which commemorates creation; for as Redemption does not destroy creation, but only removes the curse which is upon it and cleanses it from defilement, so it does not set aside its memorial, but adds a new, vivifying, and restoring element, to make the commemoration rise to its full height of excellence.

Gilfillan's statement of this argument differs in no important respect from that of other writers occupying the Puritan ground.

They all go upon the assumption of an analogy between redemption and creation so
close that each requires a Sabbath for its
commemoration. But where' is the analogy? But for the fact that the *new creation*
is represented as holding an important connection with the work of redemption, it is
doubtful whether the analogy had ever been
suspected. A new creation very naturally
suggests the old creation ; but are redemption and new creation the same thing? We
think not. Redemption is the work of
the Son of God ; the new creation is the
work of the Holy Spirit. Redemption (our
Sunday writers say) was finished by the
resurrection of Christ from the grave. The
new creation is not finished yet. It begins
with the quickening of dead souls to spiritual life. " If any man be in Christ, he is a
new creature: old things are passed away,
and all things are become new." * The

* 2 Cor. 5: 17.

growth of these souls in grace is the progress of the work, which is completed, so
far as they are personally concerned, when,
awaking in the likeness of their Saviour,
they rise from the dead. The new creation also includes that final renovation
which was foretold by the prophet,* and
which, so far from having been accomplished
by what Christ did here on earth, is yet
"looked for" by the Church according to his
promise.† When this work is finished, it
will be followed by a Sabbath,‡ but the time
is not come yet.

Redemption is the preparation and
groundwork of the new creation, but not
the new creation itself. Yet it is in this
underlying preparation that the analogy to
the work of creation is supposed to be.
But where? Save in the fact that both
works have the same Author, the resem-
blance is extremely faint. Creation was the

---

* Isa. 65: 17. † 2 Pet. 3: 13. ‡ Heb. 4: 9.

work of six days. Redemption (if the entire ministry of Christ be included) occupied three years. If redemption began
with the crucifixion, and ended with the
resurrection, it was finished on the third
day. If the ascension be accounted part of
the work, forty days more must be added.
Then where is the analogy between the two
works? Were it true that our Lord accomplished the work of redemption in the six
days preceding that of his resurrection, and
that he then rested from his work, and for
that reason blessed and sanctified that day,
the analogy would be most striking. But it
is not true. If he rested at all from his
work, it was during the time he lay in the
tomb, which (the record shows) included
the seventh day — the Sabbath.* But he

---

* In reality Christ did not rest from the work of redemption, on that
memorable Sabbath, his repose in the grave being an important part of
the work. It is not pretended, therefore, that the Sabbath gains any
thing in sanctity from this circumstance.

There was no necessity that Christ should rest, or cease, from the
work of redemption to furnish an example of Sabbath-keeping. Any

resumed the work on the morning of the day he rose, and from that hour to the present has carried it on without ceasing ; his appearance before God on our behalf* being as necessary a part of the work as his resurrection from the grave. †

---

cessation or rest on his part would have been a cessation from what was in the highest degree appropriate to sacred time. Here again the analogy between creation and redemption signally fails. In creation Jehovah wrought as an architect or builder ; his work the archetype of such employments as are lawful to man during the six working days of the week, his "rest" an example teaching that man should rest from such employments on the seventh day. In redemption it was altogether different, for the work of Christ, from first to last, was of a kind as appropriate to the Sabbath as to any other day of the week ; in fact, it was essential to true spiritual Sabbath-keeping, and, as far as any imitation of Christ is possible to his people, just the work in which we can most highly honor God on the Sabbath-day.

* Heb. 9 : 24.

† According to the law of Moses, the high-priest was not considered as having made atonement for the Israelites when he had only killed the appointed sacrifice. He was also to take the blood into the most holy place, and there sprinkle it upon the mercy seat and upon the floor before the mercy seat seven times ; and when all this was done, and not before, he was regarded as having made the atonement. (See Lev. 16th chap.) So also Christ does not complete the function for which he was constituted our high-priest by simply shedding his blood on Calvary. He must also by his own blood enter in once into the Holy Place—even into heaven itself, there to appear in the presence of God for us. For this reason we maintain that the continued presence of Christ as our Advocate with the Father is a necessary part of the work of redemption ; that the work is therefore still going on, and will not be finished till his second coming.

Following in the track of his Puritan guides, Gilfillan attempts to make Ezek. 43 : 27 speak for a change of the Sabbath under the Gospel. The prophet is describing the Temple, of which he had a vision, and our author thinks that "the only supposable accomplishment of the vision is in the condition of the Christian Church."* How that may be we do not know; for we confess that all this part of Ezekiel's prophecy is very dark to us, and we should never think of appealing to it for proof texts, unless we were sorely straitened to find them elsewhere. But he adds, "And what is there that fulfills the following prediction, if not the first day of the week and its Christian worship? 'And when these days are expired, it shall be, that upon *the eighth day, and so forward*, the priest shall make your burnt-offerings upon the

---

* Page 302.

altar, and your peace-offerings ; and I will accept you, saith the Lord."

To this we have only to reply, that whether "the eighth day" means the first day of the week, depends upon the time from which the reckoning is begun. If the priests were to begin the work of cleansing the altar on the first day of the week, then the eighth day would fall, of course, upon the next first day. But who knows whether they were to begin their work then, or upon some other day ? This is an important item in the calculation, which such writers always forget to establish. But not to waste words on this point, we submit whether the fair and natural construction of the language is any thing but this : that 'when these days— the seven days which the priests were to spend in purifying the altar—are expired, it shall be that upon the eighth day, and *every day thereafter*, the priests shall make your offerings,' etc.—the expression "and so forward," indicating that the offerings were thenceforward to be made daily.

In the use which Gilfillan makes of Col. 2 : 16-17, there is a continual begging of the question throughout. "The word in the original for Sabbath-days is plural, and always in that form has the sense of the Jewish Sabbath in the New Testament. In its singular form it is employed with the same meaning, only two exceptions being pleaded.for, in which it is supposed by some to denote the Christian Sabbath."* By the "Jewish Sabbath" our author means nothing more nor less than the seventh day of the week ; for by this misnomer he calls the Sabbath of creation. Apparently the object of this assertion is to create the impression that the word is never used in the singular when the *Jewish* Sabbath (as he invidiously terms it) is the subject of discourse. But the reader may as well be told

* Page 303.

the contrary of this ; and if he will take the trouble to refer to Matt. 12 : 2, 8, Mark 2 : 27, 28, Luke 6 : 1, 5, 6, 7, and 13 : 14, and 23 : 54, John 5 : 16, 18, and 9 : 14, 16, Acts 18 : 4, he will find in every one of these places the term used in the singular number ; and that the reference in these places is to the seventh day of the week there can be no question. The truth is that, in the New Testament, the singular and plural forms of the word are used interchangeably.

In the passage under consideration, the word is indeed plural, but the reference is not to the seventh day of the week, notwithstanding our author says, " Whether we consider the relation of the words to the Apostle's subject and purpose, the connection of confessedly Jewish ceremonies with the Sabbath-days in the verse, or the meaning of this term itself, we must believe that the Colossian converts, and, by parity of reason, all Christians, were by this sentence of

the Apostle exempted from the obligation
of keeping the seventh day Sabbath, as
really as they were from that of paying regard to the distinctions in food, the festivals,
and new moons of the preceding economy."
Before writing a dozen lines farther, however, he says, " The text relates to ritual
matters alone—to Sabbaths, as, like new
moons and holidays, forming a part of the
Jewish ceremonial." We accept this last
declaration as the key to the true interpretation of the passage. And because " the
text relates to ritual matters alone," *therefore* it has no reference to the observance
of the seventh day; for sabbatizing on the
seventh day of the week was not foresha-
dowing Christ, •it was simply commemora-
ting the finished work of creation. It was
doing what men were in duty bound to do,
had sin never entered the world.

Certain it is that, if the Apostle in this
passage had any reference to the seventh

day of the week, he had reference to the
entire institution of a weekly Sabbath.
For, as has been shown already, the notion
of the Sabbath being independent of the
day on which it is observed, is a sheer fallacy; so that a transfer of the Sabbath from
the seventh to some other day of the week
is a complete destruction of the institution.
It is not true that the institution is one
thing, and the day to be observed quite another; they stand or fall together.

In this view, then, we remark that the
Sabbath-days, of which the Apostle speaks,
were those *annual* (not weekly) seasons of
rest which by the law of Moses were connected with the great festivals of the Israelites. There were seven of them in all.
The first two were the first and seventh
days of the paschal feast. The third was
the Day of Pentecost. The fourth was the
first day of the seventh month—the Feast
of Trumpets. The fifth was the great Day

of Atonement. The sixth and seventh were the first day of the Feast of Tabernacles and the day following the close of that Feast. The law for each of these seasons was, " Ye shall have a holy convocation ; ye shall do no servile work therein."

Besides these were the sabbatical year — every seventh year, when the land was to remain untilled—and the year of Jubilee.

These sabbaths are clearly distinguished from the Sabbath of the Decalogue ; for while the latter is called " the Sabbath of the Lord," " my Sabbaths," " my holy day," and the like, the former are designated as "your Sabbaths," "her Sabbaths," etc.* The following passage is decisive on this point : " These are the feasts of the Lord, which ye shall proclaim to be holy convocations ... BESIDES the Sabbaths of the Lord."†

---

* See Exod. 20 : 10 ; 31 : 13 ; Isa. 58 : 13, and compare Lev. 23 : 24, 32, 39 ; Lam. 1 : 7 ; Hosea 2 : 11.

† Lev. 23 : 37, 38, and compare verse 3.

Quite as decisive is the language of Isaiah ; for, speaking of these annual sabbaths in connection with the whole ritual service, that prophet presents them in a light very different from that in which he presents the Sabbath of the Lord.*

These were the Sabbaths contained in that "hand-writing of ordinances," which was a shadow of things to come ;" while the weekly seventh-day Sabbath was written upon stone by Jehovah's own finger, and with all the other commandments of the Decalogue laid under the Mercy-Seat as constituting the foundation of God's throne. These annual sabbaths, together with the entire system of which they were a part, were against the Colossian brethren and contrary to them, as they were against and contrary to all other Gentiles, while the Sabbath of the Lord is not, and never was, against any. It was made FOR man. (Mark

---

* See Isa. 1 : 13, and compare chap. 56: 1-7, and 58: 13, 14.

2 : 27.)* It is certain, moreover, that the weekly Sabbath did not originate in the grace of God to sinners; for it was instituted before man had fallen. It is therefore no part of that system which foreshadowed the Saviour of sinners.

"The resurrection of our Lord from the dead was both the indication and the cause of· the transference of the sabbatic day from the end to the beginning of the week. All the evangelists record the fact that the former event took place on the first day of the week; but one of them more concisely and directly: 'Now when Jesus was risen early the first day of the week, he appeared first to Mary Magdalene.' It was not by accident that the Redeemer rose from the dead on that day. There are reasons for the times of much less important events."*

* The object of the Apostle evidently is to relieve the Gentile converts of a burden. But why should the observance of the seventh be a greater burden than the observance of the first day of the week?

† Page 308.

We agree with the author that "it was not by accident that the Redeemer rose from the dead on the first day of the week." No doubt he had a definite object in view when he chose that day, in preference to any and all others, as the time for leaving the tomb. But that his object was to make the day sacred, or to signify "the transference of the sabbatic day from the end to the beginning of the week," is not in the record: it is a mere conjecture, unsupported by a particle of proof. He must rise from the dead *some* time: was it impossible for him to rise without conferring upon the day of his resurrection a *sabbatic* character? Yet this is just what the author's argument means, if it has any meaning at all. But let us see whether the Gospel narrative throws any light upon this question.

The resurrection of Christ being the point upon which the validity of his death as a sacrifice for sins turns, it was necessary that all the circumstances of it be verified in the most exact manner. Any defect here had been fatal to the credibility of the Gospel. Two things were necessary: 1, to put the proof upon grounds which could not be controverted by his enemies; 2, to furnish this proof to his chosen witnesses before they should lose all hope, and relapse into infidelity.

Both of these requirements were met by his resurrection on the first day of the week. For as this day was the third from his crucifixion,* and as the Sanhedrim, by sealing the sepulchre's door and posting a guard of soldiers there, had taken the strictest precaution to prevent deception, intending no doubt after the expiration of the appointed three days to bring forth the body and triumphantly announce that his predictions had failed to be accomplished; and as, notwithstanding this

* Luke 24: 21.

precaution, the body was gone from the sepulchre and could not be found; so that very first day of the week—that third day from the crucifixion—furnishes proof of Christ's resurrection, under which his murderers and blasphemers are compelled to be silent. For notwithstanding the clumsy story about the body being stolen, they soon tire of telling it; never once advert to it on those trials of the Apostles which took place at Jerusalem on account of their open proclamation of their Master's resurrection; never summon any of the guard as witnesses to confront the Apostles and shame them out of their adherence to the imposture; on the contrary, an influential member of the Sanhedrim advises forbearance toward the witnesses of the resurrection, and intimates even the possibility of the event itself. (Acts 5 : 33-40.)*

But the second point—the early relief

* Morrison's Counsels to Young Men.

and satisfaction of the disciples, whose hopes had been blasted by the crucifixion of their Master—was quite as important. They were now in a despondent state. Their feet were almost gone; their steps had well-nigh slipped. They had hoped that it was he who was to redeem Israel.* But that hope was dead. They had thought that he was the Christ, the Son of the living God; but they must have been mistaken. Still they affectionately remember him as a *prophet*, mighty in word and deed before God and all the people; yet unless this feeling were encouraged by his early reappearance, how long would it be before they would forget all his wonderful works, and, like his enemies, ascribe them to collusion with Beelzebub? † It was important therefore to reassure them and establish them in the faith as soon as possible. It was by the· resurrection of

* Luke 24 : 21.   † Matt. 12 : 24.

Christ from the dead that they were begotten again to a living hope.*

It would thus appear that the real object of Christ in choosing the first day of the week as the time for rising from the dead and showing himself to his disciples was—not to signify that they had a new Sabbath-day, but—to assure them of the fact of his resurrection, according to what he had repeatedly told them. What is there in all the circumstances recorded to show that he had any other design whatever? his repeated appearances indicate no other object. Whatever he did—whatever he said to his disciples—on that day looked simply to this end. He said, "Peace be unto you. Why are ye troubled? and why do thoughts arise in your hearts? Behold my hands and my feet, THAT IT IS I MYSELF." And it is a wild conceit that makes such language equivalent to saying, 'Remember

* 1 Pet. 1 : 3.

the day to keep it holy.' And though he breathed on them, and said, " Receive ye the Holy Ghost," and conferred on them the power to remit sins; still not a word does he utter—not a hint does he give—that the day is to be henceforth held sacred. And though he appears to them again the next Sunday—for our author and all others of his stamp maintain that the expression, "after eight days," means the next first day of the week—still it is for the purpose of assuring those who still doubt of his resurrection, and for this purpose *only*, so far as appears from the narrative.

But our author does not venture the assertion that the meeting of the disciples on the day of the Lord's resurrection was held for the purpose of honoring that event. On this point he says nothing directly, though his argument for the first day of the week, taken as a whole, is so constructed as to give the impression that, from the very first, the day was set apart to commemorate that fact. Nevertheless he well knows that, on the day in question, whatever was the fact with regard to subsequent Sundays, the disciples did not come together from any such motive; for up to the time of their meeting, they did not believe that the Lord had risen.

Now, we put it to the author—we put it to every Sunday observer—whether another instance can be found in the Bible of an institution, ordinance, or festival being divinely appointed, without previous plain notification of the appointment, so that those upon whom the observance of it devolves may understand what is required of them, and what the ordinance, institution, or festival is to commemorate. At the first observance of the Passover, every Israelite knew that the Feast had been divinely commanded. When he went about killing the paschal lamb, he knew what he was doing—why he did so—what object he had in view. When that people kept the Feast of Tabernacles, they all knew that it had been appointed for them to do so, and came together understandingly, for the express purpose of doing what had been commanded. So of all other divine institutions; so of Circumcision, so of the Lord's Supper, so of Baptism. Indeed, if there is a single instance of an institution coming into existence in any other manner, it does not occur to the writer of these remarks.

Now, if the Sunday celebration of Christ's resurrection stands upon divine appointment, it is clear that the manner of its appointment was unique and exceptional. Can any good reason be assigned for this? If this institution grew up and obtained favor in a way so entirely different from any and every other, is not the presumption fair that it was "always only a human ordinance"?* Ah brethren! weak and treacherous is the ground upon which you stand here. Do you not feel it?

But what were the circumstances of the next Sunday meeting?—taking for granted that the next meeting of the disciples was on the first day of the week; though how the expression, "after eight days," proves it, was never clear to our mind. Were the disciples then assembled to commemorate their Lord's resurrection? Was that the object that brought them together? Whatever it was that brought the others, it is clear that one of their company did not meet with them from any such motive; for Thomas, up to that hour, remained an unbeliever. And there is nothing in the record to show that the reason which brought the

* "The festival of Sunday, like all other festivals, was always only a human ordinance, and it was far from the intention of the Apostles to establish a divine command in this respect, far from them and from the early apostolic church to transfer the laws of the Sabbath to Sunday."— *Neander.*

other disciples to the meeting was any thing different from that which had brought him. Our author, to be sure, *imagines* another reason, saying that " the resurrection of their Lord had prescribed the proper day, and this, with his visit, taught them to expect his presence on the first day of the week;" and that he, " by appearing among them a second time on the first day of the week, and in the scene of public worship, expresses in the most emphatic manner his approval of ' the order,' both as respects the time and the engagements of this infant Church." * But we have only to say, in reply, that this is not in the record, nor is it a necessary inference from the facts recorded.

We are now ready to consider the nature of these meetings, as determined by the situation of the disciples themselves. Gilfillan speaks of them as *religious* gather-

* Pp. 309, 310.

ings—meetings held for the avowed purpose of worshiping God. Speaking of John 20 : 26, he says, "Here we have plainly a stated day of religious convocation." But with all due deference to the author, we must say that there is no plain statement of any such thing. This, as well as the other meeting referred to, was religious in the same sense that any afternoon or evening social party is religious, when the conversation, instead of being entirely upon worldly subjects, takes a religious turn. Our reason for this view will be seen from what follows. ·

Jerusalem was not the home of the disciples. They were Galileans,* and, at the time of the Crucifixion, were temporarily resident at Jerusalem on account of the Passover. On this festive occasion, it was customary for the inhabitants to give the free use of their rooms and furniture to stran-

† Acts 2 : 7 and 13 : 31.

gers. Thus our Saviour sends his disciples
to a certain man for the use of his chamber,
which was granted at once, notwithstanding
there seems to have been no previous ar-
rangement for it.* The apartment, thus secured, was occupied by those who had taken
it as long as the festival lasted. It was their
home for the time being ; the place where
they would naturally get together in the
evening, or after the public exercises were
over, just as a family is assembled at the
evening fireside, or at supper, after the business of the day is finished. Here then is
the reason, patent, on the very face of the
narrative, why the disciples were together : because it was their common lodging
place, and not because it was a "stated religious convocation." The peculiar form of
expression, "his disciples were within," is
in perfect keeping with this idea. We call
at a neighbor's house, and inquire whether

* Mark 14: 12-16.

the family is *within;* meaning, Is the family *at home?* On this occasion, the disciples being " within," that is, *at home,* Jesus takes the opportunity to show himself.

Now, we are confident that this explanation, the verisimilitude of which is not affected by the fact that one of the meetings in question may possibly have occurred in the day-time instead of the evening, will commend itself to the reader as neither forced nor far-fetched, but perfectly natural. Nevertheless, the prejudice which clings to a long cherished notion will cling to the fact that the disciples' intercourse with the Saviour and with one another, on the occasions referred to, was of a religious character; that Jesus manifested his presence, that he said, Peace be unto you, that he encouraged their hearts, and breathed on them, and said, Receive ye the Holy Ghost, etc.—of which circumstances Gilfillan has made large capital—and so will shrink from the light which disturbs it, retreating into the dark cavern of tradition and settling back into its wonted stagnation.   But one word with you, reader, before you go.   If the religious features of the meetings referred to prove that they were regularly appointed convocations for the worship of God, what about that meeting at the Sea of Tiberias—"the third time that Jesus showed himself to his disciples, after he was risen from the dead"? Did not that meeting take a religious turn? was it not one in which Peter professed undying love for the Saviour? in which Jesus said, Feed my lambs—feed my sheep—follow me?   But who will say that it was a regularly appointed meeting—a stated religious convocation?   And the idea that it was a Sabbath-day is forbidden by the employment in which the disciples were engaged. Nevertheless, if it was possible, on this occasion, for a meeting pervaded by a religious spirit to take place without having been regularly appointed, why was it not equally possible for the two Sunday meetings, narrated by the evangelist, to have taken place without regular appointment, notwithstanding the religious element that pervaded them? And if this meeting, so religious, could have taken place on a day which was not a Sabbath but a secular day, what necessity is created by the religious complexion of the Sunday meetings referred to for supposing that the day was a Sabbath-day?

Here, then, are three recorded appearances of Jesus to his disciples, at each time the interview taking on a religious character. The first "on the same day at evening, being the first day of the week;" the second "after eight days"—possibly the next first day of the week; the third at a time not specified. And the only object of these appearances, so far as we gather from the narrative, was the complete conviction of the disciples that the Lord was actually risen.

But though these interviews put on somewhat of a religious character, there is not a particle of evidence that they took place in consequence of previous appointment; no evidence of a design, on the part of the disciples, to engage in religious exercises. No religious rites are said to have been performed by the disciples, when they met; no mention is made in either of them (as in Acts 1 : 14) of "prayer and supplication," still less of celebrating the Lord's Supper, both which (we think) would have been noted as having been attended to at the first meeting, if there had been the least design to designate the day as henceforth the stated day of worship for Christians.

Of Acts 20 : 7, Mr. G. makes what he can ; nothing more, however, than other Sunday writers before him have made, unless it be the wonderful discovery that the phrase "came together" is "the common phrase for church meetings in the New Testament"!

But we can not help thinking that the great mass of Sunday writers, Mr. G. included, exhibit themselves as singularly inconsistent in pleading this text as proof for the weekly observance of the First Day, while they practically reject the still stronger proof which it affords for the weekly "breaking of bread." Insisting, almost to a man, that to break bread means to celebrate the Lord's Supper, and that that was what brought the disciples of Troas together on the occasion referred to, they yet, with a few rare exceptions, celebrate the Supper, not every first day, but whenever it suits their convenience. If they say that the text only proves that on that particular first day of the week, when the Apostle was there, the disciples broke bread, while it furnishes no proof that they did so every first day; we accept the construction, and say that the text only proves that on that particular first day they came together and held a meeting, but does not prove that they did so every first day of the week. But no candid person can look this text in the face, without admitting that here is quite as much of apostolic example for breaking bread every first day of the week, as for holding public worship. And if Christians generally can dispense with one very important part of the service belonging to the day, because it suits their convenience to do so, they must not be grieved if it suits the convenience of some others to dispense with the other part of the service.

But if the disciples of Troas assembled to break bread on the first day of the week *because* it was the first day, is it not a little strange that the prime object of their meeting should have been delayed till after midnight, thus putting over their celebration to the next day? Or was bread broken twice that night? For it will not be overlooked, that the expression occurs twice in this celebrated passage. In the 7th verse, "the disciples came together to break bread"— which was to celebrate the Lord's Supper, our first day friends say. In verse 11th, "When he therefore was come up again, and had broken bread," etc. Does the expression mean the same in both instances? On the supposition that this was simply a convivial farewell entertainment, given the Apostle by the disciples, it was quite natural that, after his long and exhausting labors, he should break bread the second time. But this supposition does not suit our brethren ; they will have it, that breaking bread means celebrating the Lord's Supper. Be it so then. But we would remind them that after the midnight interruption of the services, which brought them down-stairs in a hurry, the Apostle went up again, and broke bread, and *ate*. Ate what? The

Lord's Supper? The word sounds very much as if it had reference to a common meal.

Let those who choose discuss the question, whether this was a Saturday night or a Sunday night meeting. If the historian had reference to the Jewish method of reckoning, it was a Saturday night meeting; for at sunset on Saturday the first day of the week commenced. In that case, Paul started on his journey on Sunday morning, giving incontestable proof that he did not regard the day as sacred. But if it was a Sunday night meeting, we wish our friends would abide by their own arguments. They all tell us that the Apostle waited a whole week after his arrival, that he might be present with the disciples on their stated day of worship, the first day of the week— drawing their inference from the silence of the narrative about any meeting held in the mean time. Thus Gilfillan: "The Apostle

Paul and his friends tarried at Troas seven days, and yet the first day of the week is the only one mentioned on which the disciples came together to break bread, or on which the Apostle preached to them." "We alluded to the Apostle's conduct at Troas as a case in which other days are allowed to pass unnoticed, and public religious services are postponed till the first day of the week should come round." Well, if no meeting was held during the time of the Apostle's stay at Troas except the one of which the narrative speaks, then there was none certainly through the day on Sunday; none till evening. What had the disciples been doing through the day? Had they been at work? Be it understood, then, that the Christian Sabbath, or "stated day of worship," begins, according to the example of Paul and the disciples at Troas, at sunset on Sunday, and continues "a long while, even till break of day," after which a Christian may go on his journey.

But, seriously, do our brethren suppose that here was a delay of a whole week—that "public religious services were postponed till the first day of the week should come round"?   Are they honest in putting forth such a view?   If they are, they give the Apostle less credit for zeal than we had supposed.   True, the narrative is silent about any other meeting.   But the mere silence of the narrative is not quite conclusive; for in the same chapter we are told that the Apostle came into Greece, and there abode three months, while nothing is said about his preaching there at all.   Yet does any one suppose that he was idle all that time?   We are morally certain that he was not; though as to the particular days on which he discoursed concerning the faith, we learn nothing from the record.   So, during his abode of seven days at Troas, his well known manner renders it in the highest degree probable that he discoursed several times ; and it is quite as probable that he discoursed on the seventh day of the week, as that he did so during the light part of the first day. But whether he did or not, is not material to the main question, the divine obligation and perpetuity of the Sabbath being independent of the Apostle's procedure in this respect.

The author's remarks upon 1 Cor. 16 : 1, 2, (p. 312,) are but an assumption of the point to be proved. The confidence with which this passage of Scripture is presented, as if it were a clear reference to the collection-box of the congregation, shows the power of the imagination to see something where there is nothing to be seen. No honest critic can take this text, either in the orignial Greek or in any fair translation, and say that the phrase, "lay by him in store," implies a public collection taken when the

church is assembled for worship. What the
Apostle commanded was, that each member
of the church should, according to the condition of his wordlly affairs, lay by himself *at
home*, something for the poor saints at Jerusalem, that it might be ready upon his arrival. It was the very reverse of a public con-
tribution ; and from the fact that the benefi-
cence of each one was to be sequestered at
home, on every first day of the week, the inference is strong, if not absolutely necessary,
that a public gathering of the Corinthian
church on that day was not known by the
Apostle. If he had known of any such cus-
tom, as originating in a design to commemorate the Saviour's resurrection, how strange
that he should mention the day with such
apparent indifference ! For in his zeal to
quicken their benevolent feelings, what was
more natural than that he should remind
them how truly they would commemorate
and sanctify the day by performing an act

of charity to their poor brethren ? But he made no such appeal ; and the fair inference is, that he recognized the day as simply a common working-day.

In what the author says of Rev. 1 : 10 there is such entire lack of argument, such a complete begging of the whole question, that we are not sure whether it is consistent with self-respect to remark upon it at all. Reduced to a syllogism, it stands thus :

I. " The expression (Lord's Day) corresponds with the phraseology of the Old Testament, 'A Sabbath to the Lord,' 'The Sabbath of the Lord thy God,' and still more with the Saviour's language, 'The Son of Man is Lord even of the Sabbath-day.'"

II. The Lord's day is the first day of the week.

III. Therefore the first day of the week, the Lord's day, is the Sabbath-day. (P. 313.)

But the writer entirely omits to establish the second term of the syllogism. In a very confident way, he assumes that it " can not be reasonably questioned." Nevertheless, we do question it, and call (as we have a thousand times before) for the scriptural proof. If (as the writer intimates, and we are not disposed to deny) there is any thing in the fact that " the expression corresponds with the phraseology of the Old Testament," then the seventh day of the week, and not the first, was the Lord's day on which John was "in the Spirit." For our own part, we do not pretend to know what day John had in view, or whether any day of the week in particular ; nor is the question determinable by any thing recorded in the word of God.

Thus far we have taken for granted that the common belief concerning the time of Christ's resurrection is correct. We are not disposed to call it in question now. But this we would say: that if the first day of the week derives all its sanctity as a day of rest and devotion from the fact that Christ rose on that day, then the precise hour when he arose should be the most sacred of all the twenty-four composing the day. Moreover, *that hour* should mark the time when the Christian Sabbath begins, and at that most sacred hour Christians should be wide awake, and ready to sing the praise of Him who

> " broke the bars of death
> And rose in conquering majesty."

How unfortunate it is, then, that the Scriptures give no information as to the hour when Christ arose. Late in the day of the Preparation, as the Sabbath drew on, some of his followers had seen him laid in the sepulchre. Early on the morning of the first day of the week, he was seen alive by Mary Magdalene. (John 20 : 14.) Matthew tells us of a visit to the sepulchre, made by Mary Magdalene and the other Mary "in the end of the Sabbath, as it began to dawn toward the first day of the

week ;" but when they got there, the Saviour was risen and gone; though at what
time he had risen this evangelist does not
say.   Mark says of Mary Magdalene and
her companions, that "very early in the
morning, the first day of the week, they
came to the sepulchre at the rising of the
sun ;" but when they got there, Jesus was
risen and gone.   *When* had he risen ? Luke
narrates the visit of the women, and says
that "upon the first day of the week, very
early in the morning, they came to the sepulchre, bringing the spices which they had
prepared, and certain others with them."
But on their arrival the Saviour was gone.
At what hour he had left Luke does not
say.   John speaks of Mary Magdalene coming to the sepulchre " early, when it was yet
dark ;" but when she got there, she saw the
stone taken away from the sepulchre.   But
John gives no account of the time when
the stone was removed.

Thus, not one of the evangelists has seen fit to note the hour when the resurrection took place. It may have occurred early on what we call Saturday evening ; it may have occurred at midnight; it may not have taken place till near morning : but on this point the record is entirely silent. Now we insist upon it, that, if the resurrection gives the day any sacredness, the *hour* of its occurrence is the most sacred part of it, and the hallowed celebration of the event should include the *hour.* Certainly, at such a sacred moment Christians ought not to be asleep. But how shall they know when to be awake ?

The only proof that Jesus arose on the first day of the week lies in the fact that He is said to have risen on the *third* day from his crucifixion. (1 Cor. 15 : 4, Luke 24 : 21.) As He was crucified on the day before the Sabbath, and was seen alive on the first day of the week, His resurrection must therefore have taken place some time

within the first half of this day, supposing
the day to have begun at sunset. Yet there
is no direct unequivocal statement that He
rose on the first day of the week. Mark
16 : 9 is made to say it by the manner in
which it is punctuated. But as the punctu-
ation of Scripture is not the work of inspi-
ration, we are at liberty to place the comma
after the word "risen," instead of after
"week," and then it will be seen that all
that the text proves is that Jesus, after his
resurrection, made his first appearance to
Mary Magdalene early on the first day of
the week.

But this only proof as to the day of the
week when Jesus rose is perhaps satisfactory
to most minds. At all events, the writer of
these remarks will not attempt to invalidate
it ; he feels no interest in doing so. But he
does think it a little strange that an event,
which is supposed to have rendered the day
of its occurrence ever after sacred as a Sab-

bath, should have been ordered to take place at such an hour of the day, (or night,) as would render the celebration of it impracticable to the mass of mankind. For the hour of its occurrence, being the most solemn of the whole twenty-four, ought certainly to be signalized and made illustrious in any commemoration of the event which pretends to have in view the *time.*

Were we to say that this hour alone should be counted sacred, it might seem captious in us. Let it be admitted, then, that so grand an event as the resurrection of the Lord must have sanctified not only the moment of its occurrence, but have thrown its sanctifying influence backward to the beginning of the day, and forward to the end of it. But who can say that it did not extend even beyond these limits? Who knows but what it sanctified two days in succession? What ground is there for limiting it to one? Redemption is a far greater work than creation, it is said; then, should not more time be consecrated to the celebration of it?

This way of treating the subject may seem frivolous to some; but we can assure the reader that it is far from our intention to worry our opponents with unmeaning sophisms. We only aim to show that this Sunday celebration, whether we consider the event on which it claims to be founded, the example and instructions of Christ, or the practice of the apostles, bears not the remotest analogy to the Sabbath; and those who attempt to impose it on the consciences of others as a divine institution are doing that for which there is not the least warrant in the Scriptures of truth.

On page 531 of Gilfillan's work is a passage, the design of which is to throw contempt upon the literary pretensions of "the friends of the seventh-day Sabbath."

"In order to get rid of the Lord's day, they endeavor to show that the expression μία σαββάτων, rendered in our Bibles 'the first day of the week,' can not refer to this day, but signifies 'one of the Sabbaths,' or 'one day of the week.' But what Mark and the other evangelists call μία σαββάτων, the former designates πρώτη σαββάτον, thus determining the meaning of both expressions to be the same, the first day of the week. The females who designed to embalm the body of Jesus did not proceed to fulfill their intention till after the Sabbath, or seventh day, was over; for it is said, 'They rested the Sabbath day, according to the commandment,' and 'in the end of the Sabbath, as it began to dawn toward the first day of the week, came to see the sepulchre,' when they found Jesus was not there. It was, therefore, on the day after the seventh day, or in other words, on the first day of the week, that his resurrection occurred," etc.

The author goes on to give an extract from Dr. Wallis in reply to Mr. Thomas

Bampfield, in which the latter is made to appear to eminent disadvantage as a critic.

Now, the writer of these remarks will undertake no defense of his brethren as mer. of learning. Their scholarship, as compared with that of others, is perhaps very inferior; but it is submitted to the most scholarly, whether "first day of the week" is a literal rendering of μία σαββάτων. Is it not a constructive rendering instead? We do not ask whether the construction is true or false to the facts narrated; that is another question; but that the translation is constructive, and not literal, will not, we think, be denied by any body. Our objection to this constructive rendering is, that it tends to keep out of view the evidence, which the passages containing the phrase afford, of the continued sanctity of the seventh day of the week.

To make this point clear, suppose a person, writing the history of our late Civil

War, gives an account of the battle of Get-
tysburg, the decisive issue of which in favor
of the Union took place on the *third of
July.* If the author were a loyal citizen,
his breast glowing with patriotic pride in
the event which had made his country a
nation among the nations of the earth, he
would probably say that the battle took
place the day before Independence Day.
But a secessionist would simply say that it
happened on the third day of the month.
Now, both accounts would be strictly true to
the fact ; yet is it not evident that the secessionist, hating the idea of freedom, and
desiring to keep out of view as much as
possible that document which declares that
"all men are created equal," phrases his
language accordingly? Now we strongly
suspect that some similar feeling—some
latent hostility to the Sabbath of the Decalogue—actuated the translators of the New
Testament, when, instead of rendering μιᾷ

τῶν σαββάτων, *one day after the Sabbath*, or *the next day after the Sabbath*, which would have been the literal translation, and was the exac idea which the sacred writer intended to express, they rendered it "first day of the week." For the literal rendering would keep the idea of the Sabbath as a sacred day before the mind, whereas the constructive translation helps to put it out of view. Try it in the several passages where the phrase occurs.

John 20 : 1. "The first day after the Sabbath cometh Mary Magdalene, early, when it was yet dark." (Just before the Sabbath, she had seen Jesus laid in the sepulchre. See Mark 15 : 47.)

19th verse. "The same day at evening, being the first (or next) day after the Sabbath, came Jesus, and stood in the midst," etc.

Acts 20 : 7. "The next day after the Sabbath, when the disciples. came together to break bread, Paul preached to them, ready to depart on the morrow."

1 Cor. 16 : 1, 2. " Concerning the collection for the saints . . . upon the first day after the Sabbath, let every one of you lay by him in store, as God hath prospered him."

Matt. 28 : 1. " In the end of the Sabbath, as it was dawning into the first day after the Sabbath, came Mary Magdalene, and the other Mary, to see the sepulchre."

Mark 16 : 1, 2. " And when the Sabbath was past, Mary Magdalene, and Mary the mother of James, and Salome, had brought sweet spices, that they might come and anoint him. And very early in the morning, the first day after the Sabbath, they came unto the sepulchre."

Luke 23 : 56, and 24 : 1. " And they returned, and prepared spices and ointments, and rested the Sabbath-day, according to the commandment. And upon the first day

after the Sabbath, very early in the morning, they came unto the sepulchre, bringing
the spices."

With this literal (or as nearly literal as
possible) translation of the phrase in question, who does not see that the Sabbath is
recognized as the sacred day—the true day
of rest? And who, that had never heard
of the Sunday celebration, on reading these
texts, thus literally rendered, would suppose
that they argued any thing at all for the
sacredness of the first day of the week?

Our author undertakes to fortify his position as to the sacredness of the first day of
the week by an appeal to ecclesiastical history. We shall not follow him in this
direction, notwithstanding we are confident
that, even here, the Bible Sabbath has nothing to fear. But in matters of religion
history is not our guide. The only question
that really concerns us is, What saith the
Scripture? Church history is, in a large de-

gree, the history of error and folly. From the days of the Apostles, the proneness of men to depart from the simplicity of the Gospel has been constantly manifested. The great antiquity of the Sunday festival need have no weight with any one who receives the Bible as his only guide. Even in Paul's day there were some who preached "another gospel;" yet any one who thus preached was not to be countenanced, though he were an angel from heaven. The Sunday celebration, though it could be traced back to the time when this anathematized error concerning the way of salvation was such a trouble to the Church, would not on that account have any stronger claim upon our regard. If not sanctioned by the Scriptures, it is to be rejected, though it were enjoined by an angel from heaven.